KU-788-200

MAISIE PARADISE SHEARRING

Bunk

with NESS WOOD

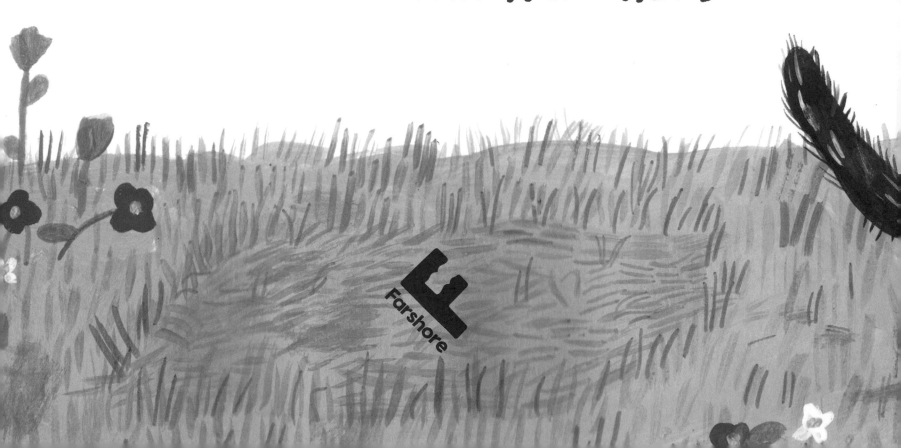

Farshore

Hello, my name's Bob!

I live in a house.

Inside is where I like to be.

At the start of the day I know just what to do,

so my breakfast is ready on time.

I'm Bunk!

I live outside in the wild.

I call the garden my home.

I wake up with the sun and enjoy the view.

The search for my breakfast is part of the fun!

Who's this?

A cat!

What's that?

A cat!

Hi, I'm Bob!

Hi, I'm Bunk!

How do you spend your day?

Well, I like a chin rub,
and to curl in a ball.
I choose the best spot
on the sofa.

If my owner eats yogurt,
I polish the bowl.

I never get fleas,
I'm incredibly clean.

Well, I bask in the sun,
and I roll in the soil.
I drink rainwater fresh
from the puddles.

I like watching bees,
but I don't get too close!

If I hear a bird
singing,
I prick up my ears.

You're lazy, like me!

I'm a dreamer like you!

We're different, but similar too!

I yeowwl for my pals, Clods, Nuts and Spider!

We get up to our usual tricks!

We chase after squirrels and bounce in the leaves,

and stare at Zazoo
when she's eating
her tea.

I wake up from a nap and I sharpen
my claws on the fanciest thing I can find.

I've got lots of nice toys, but I like this old box.

Then I umpire the tennis . . .
Breep, I've just seen a moth!

You're silly like me!

OK!

hrrumph!

meep!

purr!

The indoors is fun!

Outside feels new!

meeiowp!

We're different,

but similar too.